W9-AFS-845

CHILDREN'S AND PARENTS SERVICES
PATCHOGUE-MEDFORD LIBRARY

# Disney's
# A Winnie the Pooh First Reader

# Pooh
# Gets Stuck

ADAPTED BY Isabel Gaines

ILLUSTRATED BY Nancy Stevenson

DISNEP
PRESS

NEW YORK

Text © Disney Enterprises, Inc.

All rights reserved. No part of this book may be reproduced or transmitted in any form or by any means, electronic or mechanical, including photocopying, recording, or by any information storage and retrieval system, without written permission from the publisher. For information address Disney Press, 114 Fifth Avenue, New York, New York 10011-5690.

Printed in the United States of America.

Based on the Pooh stories by A. A. Milne (copyright The Pooh Properties Trust).

First Edition

3 5 7 9 10 8 6 4

This book is set in 18-point Goudy.

Library of Congress Catalog Card Number: 98-84172

ISBN: 0-7868-4184-2

For more Disney Press fun, visit www.DisneyBooks.com

# Pooh
# Gets Stuck

Winnie the Pooh was hungry.

Hungry for honey!

Now, honey rhymes with bunny.

And bunny means rabbit . . .

So Pooh set off to visit

his good friend Rabbit.

Rabbit always had honey

at his house.

"Come in, Pooh," said Rabbit.

"You're just in time for lunch."

That's just what Pooh

was hoping to hear.

He squeezed in through

Rabbit's front door.

Pooh sat down

at the table

and began to eat.

Pooh ate and ate.

And then he ate some more.

7

At last, Pooh stood up

and patted his tummy.

"I must be going now," he said

in a rather sticky voice.

"Good-bye, Rabbit."

Pooh started out the door . . .

And then he stopped!

Pooh's head was already outside.

But his feet were still inside.

His big, round tummy

was stuck in the middle.

Rabbit gave Pooh a push.

Rabbit gave Pooh a poke.

Nothing seemed to help.

Pooh stayed where he was.

"There is only one thing to do,"

Rabbit said.

And off he went to find

Christopher Robin.

Pooh waited for Rabbit to return.

He waited and waited.

Finally, Rabbit came back
with Christopher Robin.
Christopher Robin
patted Pooh's head.
"Silly old bear," he said.

Christopher Robin took hold

of Pooh's paw.

Rabbit took hold

of Christopher Robin's shirt.

Then they pulled

as hard as they could.

But poor Pooh stayed stuck.

"There's only one thing to do,"

Christopher Robin told Pooh.

"We must wait for you

to get thin again.

Thin enough to slip

through Rabbit's door."

So Pooh and the others waited.

After a while Eeyore came by.

He looked at Pooh and sighed.

"This could take days,"

Eeyore said.

"Or weeks," he went on.

"Or maybe even months."

"Oh, bother," said Pooh.

"Oh, bother," Rabbit agreed.

Pooh soon got tired of waiting.

Pooh was not happy.

He was hungry!

He got hungrier and hungrier
each day.

That night Gopher popped up

outside Rabbit's hole.

He opened up a big lunch box.

"Time for my midnight snack,"

Gopher told Pooh.

"Snack?" Pooh said hungrily.

19

Inside, Rabbit heard voices.

He jumped out of bed.

Rabbit did not want

Pooh snacking.

He wanted Pooh thin!

He wanted Pooh gone!

Rabbit ran out the backdoor.

Just in time.

Gopher was about to give Pooh

some honey.

"No, no, no!" Rabbit cried.

"Not one drop!"

Rabbit grabbed the honeypot.

Then he made a sign

and stuck it in the ground.

The sign read:

DO NOT FEED THE BEAR

23

Days passed.

Nights passed.

Pooh was still stuck.

Then one day, it happened.

Rabbit leaned against Pooh,

and Pooh moved.

But just a bit.

Rabbit raced off

to get some help.

Rabbit returned with Eeyore,

Kanga, Roo, and

Christopher Robin.

Christopher Robin grabbed

Pooh's paws.

Kanga grabbed Christopher Robin.

Eeyore grabbed Kanga.

Roo grabbed Eeyore.

27

Rabbit ran inside

and pushed Pooh's legs.

The others pulled his paws.

Push!

Pull!

Push!

Pop!

Pooh flew out of the doorway

and crashed into a hollow tree.

A honey tree!

Eeyore looked up at the tree.

Pooh's legs were waving

in the breeze.

"Stuck again," Eeyore sighed.

"Don't worry,"
Christopher Robin
called up to Pooh.
"We'll get you right out."

But Pooh was in no hurry.

There was honey above him.

Honey below him.

Honey all around him.

"Take your time,

Christopher Robin,"

Pooh called down.

"Take your time!"

CHILDREN'S AND PARENTS SERVICES
PATCHOGUE-MEDFORD LIBRARY

JUN 0 9 1999